DATE DUE

Demco No. 62-0549

Flights of Fancy

Flights of Fancy

And Other Poems

MYRA COHN LIVINGSTON

MARGARET K. McELDERRY BOOKS
New York
Maxwell Macmillan Canada
Toronto
Maxwell Macmillan International
New York   Oxford   Singapore   Sydney

For Bill Golden

Margaret K. McElderry Books   Maxwell Macmillan Canada, Inc.
Macmillan Publishing Company   1200 Eglinton Avenue East
866 Third Avenue   Suite 200
New York, NY 10022   Don Mills, Ontario M3C 3N1

Macmillan Publishing Company is part of the
Maxwell Communication Group of Companies.
First edition
Printed in the United States of America
10 9 8 7 6 5 4 3 2 1
The text of this book is set in 11-point Palatino.
Library of Congress Cataloging-in-Publication Data
Livingston, Myra Cohn.
Flights of fancy and other poems / Myra Cohn Livingston. — 1st ed.
p.   cm.
ISBN 0-689-50613-9
1. Children's poetry, American.   I. Title.
PS3562.I945F58   1994   94-14476
811.54—dc20

Summary: A collection of forty original poems, ranging in
subject from a bicycle lane and a dance rehearsal
to airplane seat belts and huckleberries.

"Prayer for Earth" first appeared in *The Big Book for Our Planet*, Dutton
Children's Books, 1993. "Bird Watching" first appeared in a math
anthology, *Math in Action*, Grade 5, Macmillan / McGraw Hill, 1993.
"Checkers" first appeared in a math anthology, Math in Action,
Grade 6, Macmillan / McGraw Hill, 1993.

CONTENTS

Flights of Fancy

AFTER CHRISTMAS

Back in the box
go the sun, the moon,
a glittering angel
playing a tune
on her golden harp;
a cuckoo clock,
a hummingbird,
Santa Claus with
his white glass beard;
a purse of beads,
a hunting horn
hung on the tree
before I was born;
balls of silver,
green, and red,
shimmering icicles
made of lead;
back in the box
until next year
and, resting
on top,
one
Christmas
star.

BICYCLE LANE

This bicycle lane
runs along in my mind
on the right of my head
with a street left behind

filled with houses and sidewalks
and fenced-in front yards,
but I'm on my bicycle
pedaling hard

into treetops and sky clouds
and faraway lands
where no one can find me.
I'm turning—no hands—

and yet I keep steering
and still I go on
wheeling through night
to the edge of the dawn

riding along
on the right of my mind
on a bicycle lane
with a world left behind.

BIRD WATCHING

Up in the bush is a tiny nest.
That's where the hummingbird likes it best.

Out in the trees the mockingbirds call.
Three built nests just over the wall,

And in the morning, yesterday,
I saw four crows and two blue jays.

Those were the birds I counted——ten.
Will ever the same birds come again?

BUILDING NEW YORK

I have
arranged the blocks
into a city.

Some I
have painted red,
some gray, some white.

I have
made the East River
into a mirror

and Central Park
into a forest
of green.

Across the river
I have built bridges
to little cities.

But my city
is the tallest, the biggest,
the best.

BULLFROG QUARRY

Near the brook, a porcupine
climbed up a tree. The branch of a pine

blocked our path. You bent the bough.
I scrambled up the hill somehow,

following the shadowed trail.
I thought I saw a furry tail

behind the wall where water stood
in Bullfrog Quarry within the wood.

We looked for frogs, we poked around
and listened for some splashing sounds

but all was still. We walked away.
We found a feather. We saw a jay.

A tree toad jumped across the trail.
You saw what you thought might be quail.

I searched the skies for a hovering hawk.
It was good that day, our Sunday walk

through woods and meadows and August sun,
but I never saw bullfrogs. Not a one.

BUS RIDE TO KINGSTON

I name you
                yellow creeper
                        cloud flower
        purple steeple
                flying star

                parading the road,
                sun bathing on hills,
                hiding in forest shade.

One day
I will find your true names.
It is enough, now,
that you bloom.

CHECKERS

What if
every time
you came
we would play the same old game
and the score was just the same?

I'd win one
and you'd win three.
That is how it seems to be
but for the
possibility

that if
I figure out a way
and find some better moves to play
why—
I'll be beating you one day!

8

DANCE REHEARSAL

Jacques d'Amboise and the National Dance Institute
La Guardia High School, May 16, 1992

You're waiting
in the wings—
you got that, guys?
You're in the theater now.
Give me your eyes.

Here we go—
get ready!
Make sure you're fitting in!
Five, six, seven,
five-six-seven—swing——

Up, up, everyone!
Keep the first step small.
Think hard.
Don't rush.
Wait by the wall,

and one,
two and three,
three, four and five—
make sure you're fitting in.
Give me your eyes!

I don't want to stop you.
Your arms are a mess.
No, no, no!
Please
make me say yes!

Stamp those feet.
Do it again.
Up, up,
everyone,
every single arm.

Your tap came off?
What will you do?
Don't
stop counting,
One and two——

You're on stage now.
Give me your eyes.
You're dancing,
dancing!
You got that, guys?

DEER IN NOVEMBER

Watching your black
  silhouette,
        sharp against
        the cold evening sky,
        I reach for a pair of silver scissors
          to   cut
          you   out

ELEGY FOR A DOG

I am sad
that he is gone.
I sing myself a humming song
when I wake up,
and all day long.

I sing it to
my own sad tune.
I made it up one afternoon.
The notes cry out
into my room.

I think about
the day he came,
how I decided on his name,
why, now, my life
won't be the same.

I think about
his ears and nose,
his long soft hair and all of those
funny bumps
beneath his toes.

I sit and stare
into the sky.
I try to think of reasons why
he couldn't live
and had to die.

I am sad
that he is gone.
I sing myself a humming song
when I wake up,
and all day long.

FACE IN THE CLOUDS

This cloud face, a man
with graying hair, kept staring
at me in the plane,

his eyes melting and
his beard loosening into
the air all around,

until five minutes passed
when we lost him, still smiling
in the Kansas sky

FACES

I must throw away sad.
Sad will never save me.

I must pick up happy,
Smear it with Krazy Glue.

Sad goes into the trash.
Happy stays on my face.

FLIGHT OF FANCY 1
[Flight 19, August 24]

About
the time we hit
the Mojave I jumped
out. There was a big patch of huge,
fleecy,

white clouds,
soft enough to
hold me, so I fell in,
bounced around for a while and then
eased down

into
the sand. I stayed
under the shade of clouds,
waved good-bye to the plane, started
walking

at high
noon. It's dark now
and I am still going.
Indio and Desert Mirage
are straight

ahead
where someone will
give me water and a
bed for the night. Then, tomorrow
I'll start

out for home.
I should reach there
in a few days when I'll
write and let you know what I've been
doing.

FLIGHT OF FANCY 2
[In December]

This time
I'm hopping out
into the snow

where I'll
lie down and kick
my feet to make

a skirt
and move my hands
to make some wings

and when
I jump up, there
on the cold ground

you'll find
that I have left
the white imprint

of an
angel to watch
you walking out

through the
snow and winter
at Olive Bridge

FLYING INTO NEW YORK

Clouds are busy
hiding the city,
the water,

piling up,
rushing along in
a pack,

bunching together
over summer at
Rockaway Beach.

FOR MARGOT TOMES, ARTIST

Over
and over you
draw yourself, a child with
wispy hair, skating on thin ice,
waving

a flag
against strong storms,
holding an umbrella
against chill winds, gazing backward
to strange

talking
forests, over
and over, knobby knees,
hands in your pockets, standing straight,
your feet

planted
onto a page,
meeting the world with a
wistful gaze, holding a sharp, black
pencil.

FOREST IN SUMMER: A WISH

To swim in green leaves,
dive into bright green waters,
float safely to shore.

GOOD FRIENDS

We stand,
catty-corner,
looking at the red light,
waiting for it to turn
yellow
and green.

Then we run,
you to me
and me to you
and then back to
your curb

where we
walk together
swinging arms, holding hands,
on the same side of
the street.

GRAND CENTRAL STATION

Trains wait
in a tunnel
of naked yellow bulbs
hanging

down like
stalactites from
caverns festooned with white
striped walls

ready
to run steel tracks
with amber dots, while the
red eye

of a
locomotive
watches, waiting to join
the race.

GREAT-GRANDMOTHER

She said she can't remember when
it was, the year that she turned ten,

but she remembers other things
like turning birch boughs into swings

and hiding in an empty lot
and all about the doll she got

for Christmas; how she learned to sew
and how she met her first real beau

and married, and when she was young
the ways she found to make life fun,

and how things change when you are old.
I can't remember all she told

except, she said, at ninety-three,
you know that what will be, will be.

HIGHWAY HAIKU

Wild branches, spilling
over the concrete wall, reach
out to touch the bus . . .

Leaning against each
other comfortably, birch
watch down the highway . . .

Hemlocks build themselves
their own dark houses, their own
tall secret castles . . .

Pines, tamed by fences,
pop their heads over to look
out at the traffic . . .

One willow escapes
to sun herself on the soft
grasses of summer . . .

HOUSEFLY IN AUTUMN

When I
was a housefly,
living inside on the
warm glass in November, sunning
myself,

careful
that no one could
swat me, buzzing around
on the window with my friends and
children,

I was
apt to be quite
noisy, a bit of a
bother, a terrible sort of
nuisance,

but now
I am watched by
a spider, living just
above the sunny window, where
she is

spinning,
quietly, a
tangled web of dry silk
to rid the room of annoying
houseflies

HUCKLEBERRIES

We hiked along in mountain air
and found green huckleberries where

they clumped around a flattened stone.
We stopped and sat there, all alone,

searching to find the ripened ones
among the leaves. In midday sun

we picked and ate them, juicy, blue;
sweet huckleberries, rock, and you.

HUGS

When you call
I hug myself
with joy.

You are not here
to hug me
so I pretend

a big hug,
a bear hug,
you, the bear

along the trail,
and me,
looking at you.

Hug, hug, hug,
again, again,
and still again.

I'M GONE

I'm gone.
Down Second Avenue
out of Detmold Park
and 48th Street
sailing in a Skyline taxi
through the Midtown Tunnel
at 36th Street
and on to JFK,
I'm gone.
I'm leaving
New York.

Have you missed me yet?

IN THE POPPER

little
yellow kernels
bunched together, warming
themselves up in a silver cage,
jostling

other
swelling yellow
kernels, rubbing shoulders,
bumping heads together, waiting
to pop!

IN THIS PICTURE

In this picture
I sketch a forest
in the afternoon,

white pines overhead,
leaves crunching
under my feet.

I am walking
looking for you
everywhere,

along the trail,
waiting in the meadow
or at the big rock,

but wherever I go
up or down
you are hidden,

so I step out
of the picture
and draw you

waiting by
Bullfrog Quarry
just as I come up the trail.

You are surprised
that I have been
looking for you

and thank me
for putting you
into my picture

and on you hike
as I sketch myself
following closely behind.

JUNE BIRDS

They are
so happy with
themselves this afternoon,
twittering somewhere in glossy
green leaves,

pitching
their highest notes
from hidden nests into
the sky and head-on into this
poem.

LETTER TO A PEN PAL

I have
just cut out all
the states from Arizona
to Pennsylvania and thrown them
away.

Now that
California
and New York are so close
we can get together most of
the time

and play
over at your
house or play here at mine
and talk whenever we want to
and ride

our bikes
and we won't need
to stay on the phone for so long
and I can stop writing all these
letters.

MARCHING BUSHES

Like armies of wooly animals
bushes march up the hill every night,
black against a pink sky;
the same parade marching from east to west, black
head and horns
silhouetted in gray dusk

These are the silent beasts who watch
my house,
who live in my mountains.
On windy nights their shaggy heads
nod in the wind.
Tonight they are quiet.

Still they speak, looking at me,
Come out and walk with us,
Climb to the top of the hill,
Be brave against the dying sun, the white moon.
March into the night.

PRAYER FOR EARTH

Last night
an owl
called from the hill.
Coyotes howled.
A deer stood still
nibbling at bushes far away.
The moon shone silver.
Let this stay.

Today
two noisy crows
flew by,
their shadows pasted to the sky.
The sun broke out
through clouds of gray.
An iris opened.
Let this stay.

SCENARIO FOR STAYING HOME
FROM SCHOOL

(I tell myself
that my throat is sore
with a sort of an itch
I had before
when I played in the rain
and caught the flu.
It isn't that bad
but
I make it do
when I go downstairs
in a shuffly way.)

Mom says: *What's wrong with you today?*

(I hang my head,
hold on to my ear
and choke a little)

Mom: *What's wrong, dear?*
Me: It's sort of my throat but more my head.
Mom: *No school for you. Go back to bed!*

SEAT BELTS OVER KANSAS

This trip Kansas hides
herself under gray blankets
and white comforters

waiting for the time
when our pilot turns off the
seat belt sign so we

can get up again
and Kansas can kick away
her heavy covers.

SPARROWS

Tiny
planes, cleared for flight,
zooming street runways, take
off from telephone-wire tower
control.

SUNSET

[A Tanka]

Now that December
has gone the sun stays on the
hilltop much longer . . .
waiting for me to climb up
and watch as it disappears . . .

TAKE OFF

I look down to find
you, to wave good-bye, but you
are not standing there . . .

even if you were
I couldn't see you through the
cover of dense clouds . . .

nor, I guess, could you
spot me in this 767
flying up so high . . .

THE PICTURE PLACE

I drew a picture.
You and I
were underneath
a summer sky

but suddenly
you ran away.
I called and asked
if you would stay

but you had
left the page and stood
outside. You never
understood

I dreamed the picture
up to be
a special place
for you and me,

a place which no one else
had known,
where we could play
and be alone.

So come back in,
Step carefully
Into my picture place
With me.

THE QUESTION

Bud is gone.
The movers came.
Things won't ever be the same.

His father
drove the car away.
They've got a house where they can stay

a long way off
in some dumb place.
No matter what I do Bud's face

comes swimming out
into my eyes.
I don't like all those other guys

who say Bud's family
had to go.
How do they know?

20/20

Below the big
E
I can see

NCBEDHG
HCEOG   and Z
BOFDC   and V

(*That's right,* they say,
and smile at me.)

WATCHING TV

I put
myself into
the stormy gray ocean,
in a leaky boat beginning
to sink

where I
have no water
left to drink, nor food to
eat, but suddenly, I spy you,
waving

to me
from a big ship,
sending out a rescue
crew to save me, and make me safe
once more.